Lots of love to Paul and Sue Davies – S.M.
For Cheryl, Louise, Petrona, and Aniyah – C.G.

tiger tales
5 River Road, Suite 128, Wilton, CT 06897
Published in the United States 2021
Text by S. Marendaz
Illustrations by Carly Gledhill
Text and illustrations copyright © 2021 Little Tiger Press Ltd.
ISBN-13: 978-1-68010-211-6
ISBN-10: 1-68010-211-7
Printed in China
LTP/2800/3504/1120

For more insight and activities, visit us at www.tigertalesbooks.com

NOTHING SCARES SPIDER!

by S. MARENDAZ   Illustrated by CARLY GLEDHILL

tiger tales

Spider was planning a big
adventure.
She was going to be an explorer.

SPIDER'S
HOUSE

"I'm going to see the Whole
Wide Yard," cheered Spider.
And she went to say good-bye
to her friends.

Caterpillar, Ladybug, and Bumblebee
thought an adventure sounded scary.

"What about the Fearsome Fish?
The Hungry Birds? And the Clever
Cat?" they asked.

Spider just laughed.
"Spiders aren't scared of
anything," she said.

"But who will protect US?"
her friends wailed.

"I'll leave a web so you can
call me back," said Spider.
"But only in emergencies."

Yum, lunch!

Spider skipped to
the Tall Tall Trees.

She wasn't scared
of Hungry Birds.

"Ha!" Spider laughed.

"What is it?" said Spider.

It was Ladybug.
"Oh, Spider!" she flapped.
"Someone's in my flower!"

"That's just Bumblebee!" said Spider.
"Phew!" said Ladybug. "Thanks!"
"This web is only for emergencies!" said
Spider. "I'm very busy with my adventure!"

And off she went.

LADYBUG'S
HOUSE

Spider skipped to the Big Blue Pond.
She wasn't scared of Fearsome Fish.

"Ha ha!" laughed Spider.
But just then . . .

— Ooh, tasty!

TWANG!

An emergency!

Spider rushed
home at once.

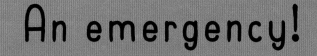

"What is it? What is it?" cried Spider.
"Oh, Spider," gulped Caterpillar. "There's
something huge and scary behind me!"
"That's just your shadow!" said Spider.

"Oh," said Caterpillar. "Silly me!"
"Caterpillar! I told you—this web is
only for emergencies!" said Spider.
"You're interrupting my adventure."
And off she went again.

Spider skipped to the Lush Long Grass. She
wasn't scared of the Clever Cat. Not one bit.
"Ha ha ha!" laughed Spider.

But just then . . .

TWANG!

It had to be an emergency this time!
Right?

"What is it now?" Spider asked Bumblebee. "Ummm . . . I heard a scary buzzing noise!" said Bumblebee.

"That's **you**," said Spider. She was starting to feel very impatient.

"Phew!" said Bumblebee. "That was close!"

Buzz
Buzz

"It **wasn't** close because there's **nothing** scary in the flowerbed. Now **please leave the web alone!**" Spider shouted, and she stomped off to continue her adventure in peace.

Spider traveled farther and farther away.

But just then . . .

YAN

Spider was tugged all the way back home
and right into—an emergency!
"The Frightening Frog is going to eat us!"
cried her friends.

HELP!

But Spider wasn't scared.

"HEY, YOU!" she shouted.

The frog turned to Spider.
His yellow eyes gleamed . . . .

EEK!

Now the Frightening Frog
was going to eat her.

And Spider was scared.
Very scared!

"Quick, Spider!" called Caterpillar. "We can stop him if we work together."

So Spider spun a web . . . and Ladybug and Bumblebee dropped it on the frog's head.

"We'll let you out if you buzz off!" they all told him.

And he did!

"Thank you for saving us," said
Spider's friends. "We tried
to be brave, like you."

"You saved **me!**" said Spider. "I guess that even spiders are scared **sometimes**. On my next adventure, you're all coming with me. In case of emergencies!"